TO:

FROM:

W9-BMP-062

ISBN 978-0-8431-7808-1

50399>

EAN

9 780843 178081

MR. FUNNY

by Roger Hargreaves

One day Mr. Funny was having lunch.

He wasn't very hungry, so he only had a daisy sandwich and a glass of toast!

"Delicious," he murmured to himself as he finished his funny lunch.

After lunch Mr. Funny decided to go for a drive in his car.

Mr. Funny's car was a shoe!

Have you ever seen a car that looks like a shoe?

It looks very funny!

As he drove along, everybody who saw him laughed at him because he was such a funny sight.

He passed a worm at the side of the road.

This worm thought Mr. Funny in his funny car was the funniest thing he had ever seen.

He nearly laughed himself in two!

Even the flowers Mr. Funny passed thought that he was the funniest thing that they had ever seen.

They nearly laughed themselves out of the ground!

Eventually Mr. Funny came to an intersection.

He didn't know which way to go, so he looked at the signs.

One of the signs said TO THE ZOO.

That will be fun, thought Mr. Funny, so he drove his shoe toward the zoo.

When he arrived at the gate of the zoo, he stopped.

It was closed.

"I'm sorry," said the zookeeper. "We've had to close the zoo because all the animals have colds, and they're all feeling very sorry for themselves."

"Oh dear," said Mr. Funny, and then he thought for a moment. "Perhaps I can help to cheer them up," he said.

"Well," said the zookeeper, "it's worth a try." And he opened the gate.

Mr. Funny drove into the zoo.

In his shoe.

The first thing he saw was an elephant. It was true.
The elephant was feeling very sorry for herself.
Very sorry indeed.

Mr. Funny looked at the sad-looking elephant.

And the sad-looking elephant looked at Mr. Funny.

Oh dear!

Then do you know what Mr. Funny did?

He made a funny face!

Mr. Funny, as you'd imagine, is very good at making funny faces.

The elephant giggled.

She'd never seen anything so funny.

Mr. Funny made another funny face.

The elephant burst out laughing.

The elephant laughed and laughed and laughed.

She laughed so hard, she nearly laughed her trunk off!

And she felt a whole lot better.

Mr. Funny went over to the lion house.

There was a lion, feeling very sorry for himself.

Mr. Funny looked at the sad-looking lion.

And the sad-looking lion looked at Mr. Funny.

Oh dear!

And then Mr. Funny made the funniest-looking face that's probably ever been made anywhere, ever.

Now, you've heard a lion roar before, haven't you?

Well, this lion roared too—with laughter.

He laughed so hard he nearly laughed his whiskers to pieces.

Then Mr. Funny went around to see all the other animals in the zoo.

Oh dear. What a miserable-looking bunch!

For all of them, Mr. Funny made funnier and funnier faces.

The big brown bear giggled, and then burst out laughing.

And the giraffe laughed so hard she nearly laughed her neck into a knot. And the hippopotamus nearly laughed himself out of his skin. And the penguins nearly laughed their flippers floppy. And the leopard—well, you really should have seen him—he laughed so hard he nearly laughed his spots off!

What craziness!

"Oh, Mr. Funny," giggled the zookeeper. "Oh, Mr. Funny, thank you very, very much for coming to cheer us up!"

"Oh, it was nothing really," replied Mr. Funny modestly, and drove off . . .

. . . in his shoe!

Later, when Mr. Funny arrived home, he chuckled to himself. "Well," he said. "That's the end of another funny day!"

And he parked his shoe and went inside his teapot and, because he was feeling thirsty, he made himself . . .

. . . a nice hot cup of cake!